ANIMALS AT
HOME
Craig Brown

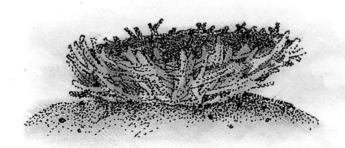

ROBERTS RINEHART PUBLISHERS

Golden eagle's
aerie

Grizzly bear's cave

Bighorn sheep's slope

Hoary marmot's doorway

Mountain lion's den

Moose's range

Badger's burrow

Hummingbird's nest

Raccoon's tree

Silver-haired bat's hole

Beaver's lodge

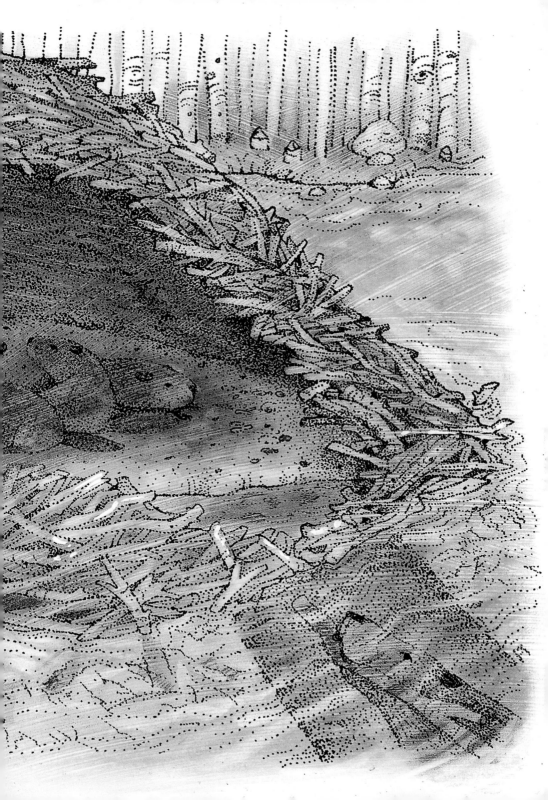

My room

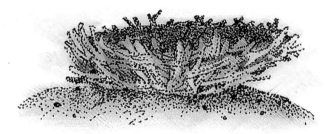

The **golden eagle's aerie (nest)** is built of tangled twigs and branches on a large or solid platform on inaccessible clifftops, or the tops of trees. The nest is used for many years with new branches being added each year during the breeding season.

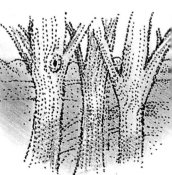

The grizzly bear's cave is a protected area where they sleep away the harshest part of winter. Their sleep is not deep and their temperature falls only a few degrees below normal. They are not true hibernators.

The silver-haired bat's hole is in protected spots such as abandoned woodpecker holes, bird nests, or under bark. These bats are solitary animals, emerging in early evening to feed. Summe are spent in the north woods they generally migrate south the winter.

Hoary marmot's doorway is one of a few entrances to its den under a debris of rock at the base of a cliff. The marmot is a true hibernator, sleeping through the long winter months until spring.

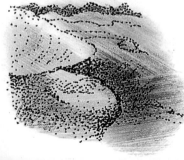

The badger's burrow is dug on mountain plateaus. Badgers become sluggish in the winter and remain in chambers deep within their burrow, but do not hibernate.

The mountain lion's den can be in a cave, rocky cliff, or any protected area, which the female will line with vegetation when she is ready to give birth to her young. The rest of the time, mountain lions will roam as far as 25 miles a day.

Moose migrate seasonally from high mountain slopes to lower valleys, and will often join other herds during winter months. In summer, the moose is solitary but may join others near lakes to feed. Bull moose will thrash brush with their antlers to mark their temporary territory.

broad-tailed humming-'s nest is built by the ale on a tree branch or a rock wall, near flowers, rovide food for herself and young. The teacup-shaped is built with grass, moss, t down and fiber, and held ther with sticky spider bing.

The beaver's lodge is built among streams, rivers, marshes, lakes, and ponds. Beavers normally incorporate a dam with their lodge. Each lodge has one or more underwater entrances, and living quarters in a hollow opening near the top. Lodges are generally built with willow, maple, poplar, aspen or birch and caulked with mud.

Bighorn sheep spend summers on rocky cliffs, high mountain slopes, and alpine meadows, retiring to a different bedding spot each night. In the winter bighorns migrate to lower valleys.

The raccoon's tree house is normally a permanent home built in a hollow tree along wooded streams, ponds or shores. It is lined with leaves by the female.

To the students and teachers of Strawberry Park
and Soda Creek elementary schools where it started,
to all the other schools visited over the years,
and to Moe, wonderful friend and companion.

ISBN 1-57098-077-2
Library of Congress Catalog Card Number 96-67083

Distributed in the United States and Canada by Publishers Group West

Printed in Hong Kong